Underpants
for Ants

Russell Punter

Illustrated by Fred Blunt

Nan sells fancy fans and lamps,

hand bells,

clam shells,

pans and stamps.

But customers just stay away.

And so she sits and knits all day.

One cold night, Nan lights a candle

and grabs a small pan by the handle.

But as she pours soup from a can...

a gang of ants leaps from the pan.

"I can help you," Nan declares.

"I have yards of yarn to spare.

I'll knit you something warm to wear."

Nan's whiskers twitch.
Her needles click.

"Handmade underpants!"
"How grand."

Soon bugs are hopping up the hill.

Nan's shop is full, and so's her till.

Nan gets a snug hug from the ants.

"Thanks for our wonderful underpants!"

About phonics

Phonics is a method of teaching reading, used extensively in today's schools. At its heart is an emphasis on identifying the *sounds* of letters, or combinations of letters, that are then put together to make words. These sounds are known as phonemes.

Starting to read

Learning to read is an important milestone for any child. The process can begin well before children start to learn letters and put them together to read words. The sooner children can discover books and enjoy stories and language, the better they will be prepared for reading themselves, first with the help of an adult and then independently.

You can find out more about phonics on the Usborne Very First Reading website, **www.usborne.com/veryfirstreading** (US readers go to **www.veryfirstreading.com**). Click on the **Parents** tab at the top of the page, then scroll down and click on **About synthetic phonics**.

Phonemic awareness

An important early stage in pre-reading and early reading is developing phonemic awareness: that is, listening out for the sounds within words. Rhymes, rhyming stories and alliteration are excellent ways of encouraging phonemic awareness.

In this story, your child will soon identify the *a* sound, as in **hand** and **lamps**. Look out, too, for rhymes such as **spare** – **wear** and **thick** – **pick**.

Hearing your child read

If your child is reading a story to you, don't rush to correct mistakes, but be ready to prompt or guide if he or she is struggling. Above all, give plenty of praise and encouragement.

Edited by Jenny Tyler and Lesley Sims

Designed by Caroline Spatz

Reading consultants: Alison Kelly and Anne Washtell

First published in 2013 by Usborne Publishing Ltd., Usborne House, 83-85 Saffron Hill, London EC1N 8RT, England.
www.usborne.com Copyright © 2013 Usborne Publishing Ltd.